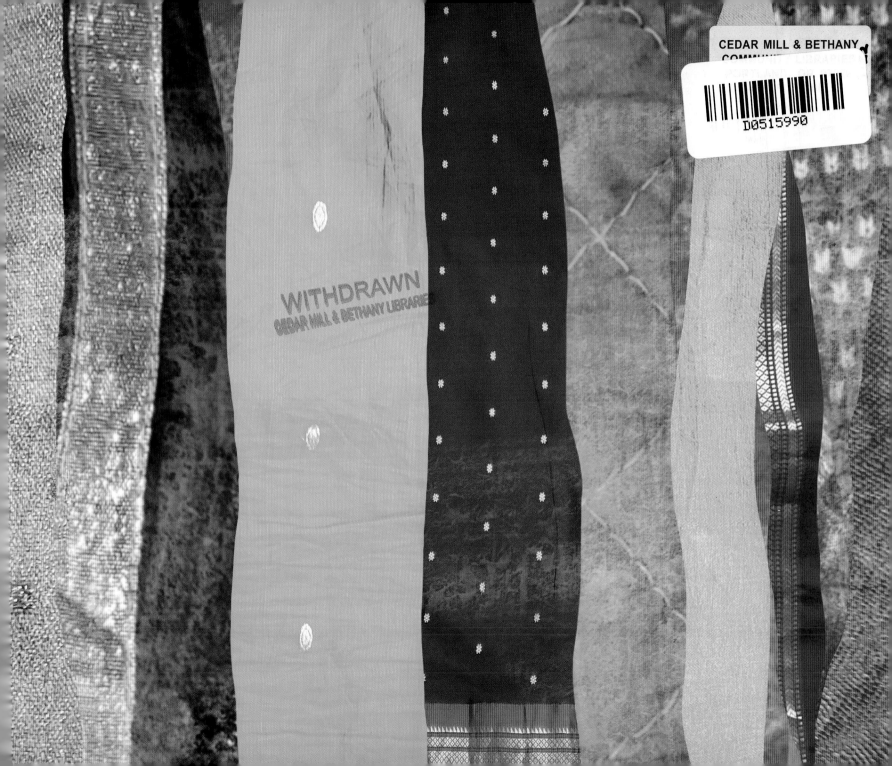

To my daughters,
Vedika and Keerti, my American desis
—JRG

To Shaan and Kathleen
—SK

ABOUT THIS BOOK

The illustrations were made with cut and torn paper, fabrics, mixed media, and digital collage, and rendered in Procreate and Photoshop. This book was edited by Esther Cajahuaringa and designed by Patrick Collins with art direction from Véronique Lefèvre Sweet. The production was supervised by Kimberly Stella, and the production editor was Annie McDonnell. The text was set in 1906 French News, and the display type is Shangri-La.

Text copyright © 2022 by Jyoti Rajan Gopal • Illustrations copyright © 2022 by Supriya Kelkar • Cover illustration copyright © 2022 by Supriya Kelkar • Cover design by Patrick Collins and Véronique Lefèvre Sweet • Cover copyright © 2022 by Hachette Book Group, Inc. • Hachette Book Group supports the right to free expression and the value of copyright. The purpose of copyright is to encourage writers and artists to produce the creative works that enrich our culture. • The scanning, uploading, and distribution of this book without permission is a theft of the author's intellectual property. If you would like permission to use material from the book (other than for review purposes), please contact permissions@hbgusa.com. Thank you for your support of the author's rights. • Little, Brown and Company • Hachette Book Group • 1290 Avenue of the Americas, New York, NY 10104 • Visit us at LBYR.com • First Edition: June 2022 • Little, Brown and Company is a division of Hachette Book Group, Inc. • The Little, Brown name and logo are trademarks of Hachette Book Group, Inc. • The publisher is not responsible for websites (or their content) that are not owned by the publisher. • Library of Congress Cataloging-in-Publication Data • Names: Gopal, Jyoti Rajan, author. | Kelkar, Supriya, 1980- illustrator. • Title: American desi / by Jyoti Rajan Gopal ; illustrated by Supriya Kelkar. • Description: First edition. | New York : Little, Brown and Company, 2022. | Audience: Ages 4-8. | Summary: An American child of South Asian descent revels in dances, clothing, games, foods and other characteristics of both cultures, while blending them into what makes this American desi unique. | Identifiers: LCCN 2020043298 | ISBN 9780316705301 (hardcover) • Subjects: CYAC: Stories in rhyme. | East Indian Americans—Fiction. | Identity—Fiction. • Classification: LCC PZ8.3.G643 Ame 2022 | DDC [E]—dc23 • LC record available at https://lccn.loc.gov/2020043298 • ISBN 978-0-316-70530-1 • PRINTED IN CHINA • APS •
10 9 8 7 6 5 4 3 2 1

American Desi

By **JYOTI RAJAN GOPAL**

Illustrated by **SUPRIYA KELKAR**

LITTLE, BROWN AND COMPANY
New York   Boston

Festive henna, garnet red
Bindis, bangles, desi queen

Fantasy hair,
seafoam green...

Which is the color of me?

Rhythmic stride, jaunty step
Jangly yellow, Bollywood moves

Shimmery blue, hip-hop grooves...
Which is the color of me?

Bell chimes, bare feet, sacred space
Flowers, incense fill the air

Wearing shoes without a care
Which is the color of me?

One foot here,
   one foot there
Straddling, bridging
   worlds apart

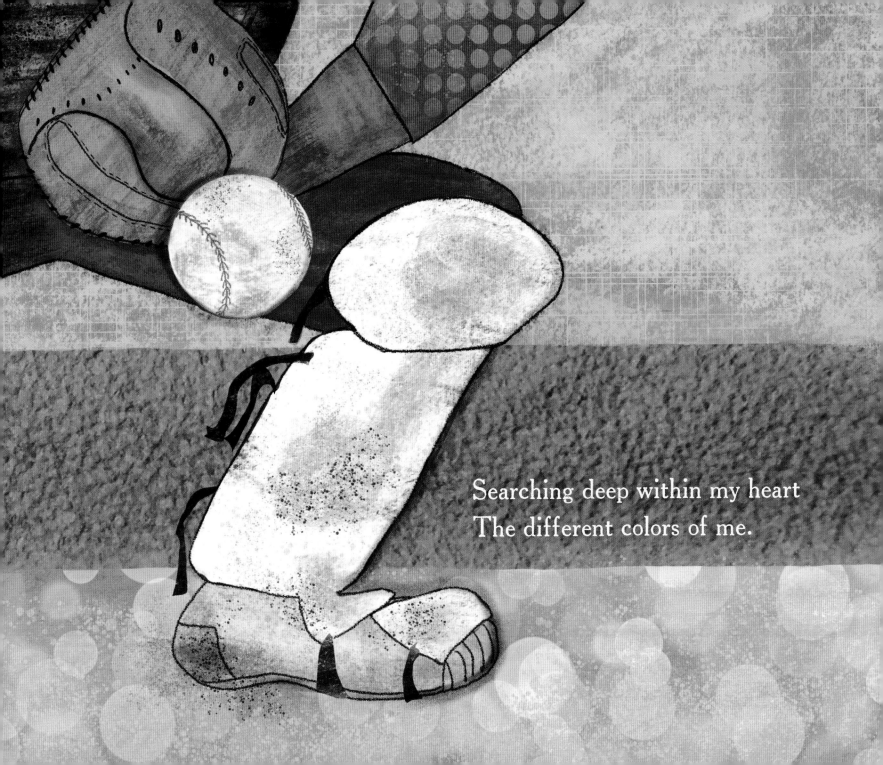

Searching deep within my heart
The different colors of me.

Cricket wickets, innings, runs
Shouts and cheers and screams for all

Football scrimmage, sacks and calls
Which is the color of me?

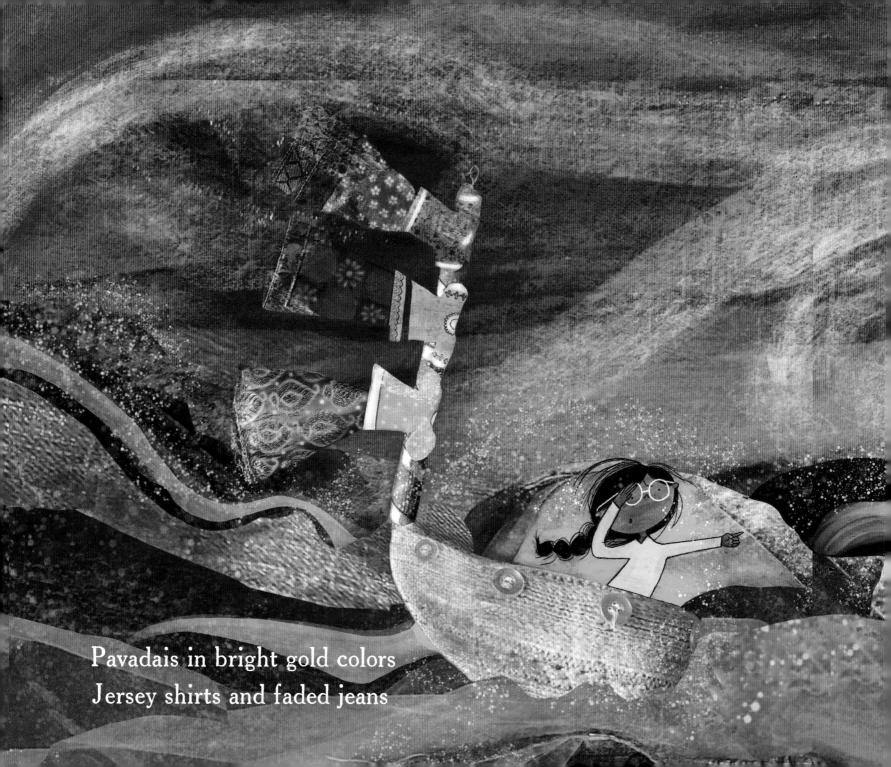

Pavadais in bright gold colors
Jersey shirts and faded jeans

Swapping, changing, feeling seen...
Which is the color of me?

Threads that spin and wind and knot
Pulling, tugging all the strands
Gathering, holding in my hands
The different colors of me.

Silky, shimmery, flowy, fancy
Lacy, crinkly, satin, plain

Twining, binding, one refrain
That shapes the fabric of me.

Hindi, Tamil twirl and swirl
English drawls and twangs and flares

One voice here, one voice there
Finding the sounds of me.

Mac 'n' cheese with fork or spoon
Dosas, idlis, fingers scoop

Spicy, tangy, savory loop
Blending the flavors of me.

Scents and accents pop and simmer
Loud and proud, my worlds collide

Forging space, no need to hide
The many colors of me.

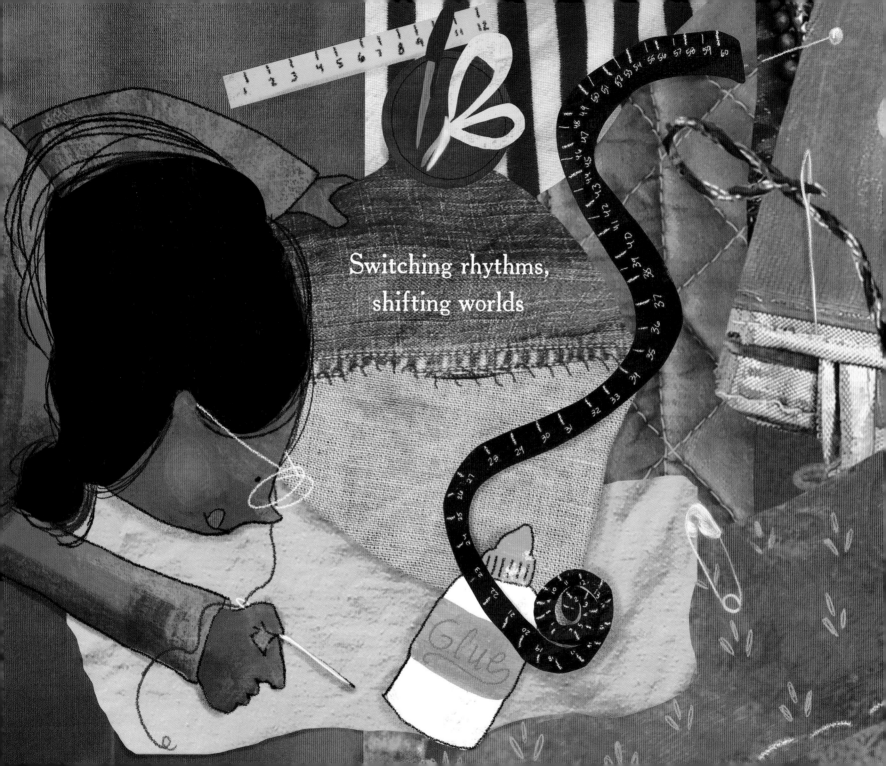

Switching rhythms,
shifting worlds

Feeling fierce,
a joyous call

Giving thanks for one and all

The wondrous colors of me.

Shedding doubts, keeping faith
Raising hope, let it sing
Blending, merging, taking wing
The glorious colors of me.

Desi fam, American roots
Guiding, holding, raise me strong

Spirit, pride, a heart-deep song...
This is the color of me.

American desi, blurring lines
Blooming, thriving, watch me grow

Staying true to *all I know*...
To all the colors of me!

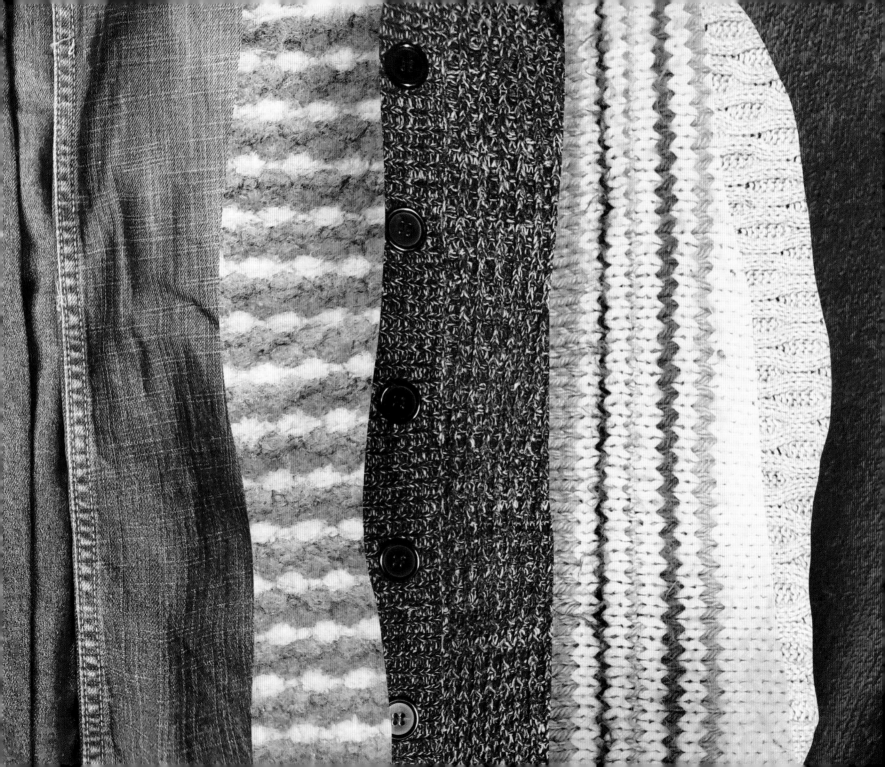